Goosebumps®

NIGHT OF THE LIVING MONSTERS

Adapted by Kate Howard
Based on the Motion Picture "Goosebumps"
Screenplay by Darren Lemke
Story by Scott Alexander & Larry Karaszewski

GOOSEBUMPS, SCHOLASTIC and associated logos are registered trademarks of Scholastic Inc.
© 2015 Columbia Pictures Industries, Inc. All Rights Reserved.
Published by Scholastic Inc., *Publishers since 1920*. SCHOLASTIC and associated logos are trademarks and/or registered trademarks of Scholastic Inc.

ISBN 978-0-545-82254-1
10 9 8 7 6 5 4 3 2 1   15 16 17 18 19
Printed in the U.S.A.   40
First printing, September 2015

SCHOLASTIC INC.

"Mom, are you sure there weren't any other towns looking for vice principals?"

Zach looked out the car window at Madison, his new hometown. The place was totally dead.

His mom pulled up in front of their new house. "Look, a yard! You'd never have something like this in New York."

Zach sighed. "I'm staying because I love you . . . and because I can't live on my own until I'm eighteen."

As Zach unpacked the car, the girl next door came by. "So, you're the new neighbor," she said.

"I'm Zach."

"I'm Hannah." She glanced over her shoulder. "I gotta go."

Before Zach could reply, she was gone.

A moment later, a man's face peeked out from behind the curtains. "Stay away from my daughter, and we won't have any problems," the man growled.

The next day at school, Zach's classmates were just as welcoming as his spooky new neighbor. People made fun of his clothes. And in chemistry, his lab partner pulled a prank that left Zach covered in yellow goo.

The only person who was nice to him was a boy named Champ. "How are you liking it here so far?" he asked.

Zach rolled his eyes. "It's everything I hoped and more."

When Zach took out the trash that night, he had a feeling someone was watching him. "Hello?" he whispered. "Is someone there?"

"Did I scare you?" Hannah asked.

"No," Zach lied. "So, is there anything fun to do around here?"

Hannah shrugged. "I'm the wrong person to ask—it's just me and my dad. I'm home-schooled."

"There's gotta be something fun you do, besides scaring your neighbors," Zach said.

Hannah shrugged. "Well, there is one thing. Come on—this way."

She led him into the woods.

"Are you taking me somewhere to kill me?" Zach asked. "Just curious."

Hannah laughed. "I'm playing it by ear, scaredy-cat."

After a few minutes, they came to a huge, abandoned amusement park.

Hannah and Zach walked around for a long time. Zach was happy he'd found a friend. But back home, the fun was over.

"Where were you?" Hannah's dad demanded.

"I'm sorry," Hannah whispered.

"Get. In. The. House. Now," her dad growled. Then he turned to Zach. "If you don't stay away from us, something very bad will happen!"

At the school assembly the next day, Zach sat alone. Champ plopped down next to him.

"How do you know that seat's not taken?" Zach asked.

"Come on." Champ grinned. "Hey, are you going to tonight's dance with anyone?"

"No."

Champ nodded. "Cool. I'm going stag, too. Maybe we should go together?"

Zach just shrugged. A school dance was not in his plans.

Later, Zach sat alone in his room doing homework. Suddenly, a scream pierced the night.

"Hannah!" Zach gasped. He rushed next door. "I heard a scream," he told Hannah's dad. "Is Hannah okay?"

"There was no scream," Hannah's dad said. "Now, get out of here—or the last scream you'll ever hear will be yours!"

Zach ran home. "Mom! Hannah's in trouble."

"Who's Hannah?" his mom asked.

But Zach was already calling 911. Then he and his mom hurried to meet the police.

"Hannah was staying with me, but she went back to her mom's yesterday morning," Hannah's dad told the cops.

Suddenly, another scream echoed from inside the house.

Zach and the police officers barged inside. An old monster movie was playing in the living room.

"Surround sound," Hannah's dad explained. "But thank you so much for stopping by. And for bringing the police."

"I'm so sorry," Zach's mom said as the cops pulled Zach out the door.

"Mom, Hannah's in trouble—I know it," Zach told her.

But his mom didn't believe him.

Zach was worried. He paced in his room. Then he saw Hannah in the window next door!

"I knew it," Zach muttered. He rushed outside—and bumped into Champ. His new friend was dressed up for the dance.

Champ eyed Zach's outfit. "Is that what you're wearing?"

"I need your help," Zach whispered. "There's this girl next door, but she's locked in the house and her dad's crazy. We need to get her out."

"This is not how I saw my night going," Champ grumbled.

Zach shushed him. Hannah's dad was getting in his car! "All right! Let's check out the house."

Zach broke the lock on the front door. He and Champ tiptoed into the hall.

A creepy sound came from above. "Let's go," said Zach.

"I agree," Champ said, heading for the door. But Zach was going up the stairs. "No, I meant go *outside*. Or anywhere else, really."

At the top of the stairs, light spilled through two closed doors.

"Hannah . . . !" Zach hissed.

The only answer was a creaking sound from behind the doors.

Zach peered inside. It was someone's office. The shelves were filled with hundreds of leather-bound manuscripts.

"That's weird," Zach said. "It's like the noise is coming from the bookcase."

"*The Scarecrow Walks at Midnight, The Ghost Next Door, Night of the Living Dummy.* These are Goosebumps manuscripts!" said Champ.

"You mean those kids' books?" Zach asked.

Champ picked up *The Abominable Snowman of Pasadena.* "No, kids' books help you fall asleep. These books keep you up all night. R.L. Stine . . . whatever happened to that guy?"

"Who knows?" Zach said. "Let's go."

Little Comic Shop of Horrors

Toy Terror: Batteries Included

Go Eat Worms

"Why are the books all locked?" Champ asked.

Zach shrugged. He noticed a key and turned it in the lock of *The Abominable Snowman*. "Mystery solved. Now, let's get back to why we're—"

Suddenly, a figure appeared in the shadows behind Champ.

"Get down!" Zach pushed Champ to the floor as a baseball bat swung at their heads.

"Zach?" Hannah asked. "What are you doing in my house?"

"I thought you were chained up, possibly," Zach said.

"You have to leave now!" Then Hannah noticed the manuscript on the floor. "Did you open that lock?"

"I—I may have?" Zach stammered. "I'll just put it back, and we'll pretend this whole thing never happened." He grabbed the book, and the cover flapped open.

"No!" Hannah screamed. "Don't open it!"

A strong, cold blast of wind knocked them all backward. Then an enormous creature burst out of the manuscript's pages. It was a real, live Abominable Snowman!

"Nobody move," Hannah whispered.

The room trembled. Manuscripts fell to the floor as the Snowman thundered toward them.

The creature leaped into the air. Then it crashed through the huge window onto the front lawn!

Hannah grabbed the *Snowman* manuscript. "My dad's gonna kill me!" She ran down the stairs and into the night.

"Hannah, wait!" Zach chased after her.

Champ grabbed him. "Listen very carefully," he cried. "That's the *Abominable* Snowman. You don't get that name by accident. And it just crawled out of *a book*!"

Zach shook him off. "I'm going after Hannah."

Zach and Champ followed Hannah across town into an ice-skating rink. She was standing in the rink, holding up the manuscript.

"What's she gonna do?" Champ asked. "Read it a story?"

"Shhh!" Hannah said. *"It's in here!"*

Suddenly, something pinged on the ice beside Zach. "It's an M&M." Another candy bounced off the ice. "Look out!"

A moment later, a vending machine crashed down, missing the kids by inches. The Abominable Snowman came down after it.

Zach and Champ ran. But Hannah didn't move.

"The only way to stop it is to suck it back in the book," she said. "I'm not close enough."

Hannah clicked open the book's lock.

The Abominable Snowman charged at her, knocking the book out of her hands.

All three kids slipped across the ice.

"In here!" Champ yelled.

Together, Champ, Zach, and Hannah slid into the penalty box. Champ slammed the door shut, and the creature crashed into it.

"Stop!" a voice shouted.

It was Hannah's dad! He opened the manuscript, and the book sucked the creature back between the pages.

Hannah's dad slammed the book shut. "All of you, in the car—now!"

"Dad, they were only trying to help," Hannah whispered.

"I told you if you didn't stay away from us, something bad would happen. You had to pick *Abominable Snowman of Pasadena*? You couldn't have picked *Little Shop of Hamsters*?"

That's when Zach realized something. "You're R.L. Stine, aren't you? The author of Goosebumps?!"

Back home, Zach had a million questions for R.L. Stine.

"Go home!" Stine told him.

"No. Not until you explain what's going on," Zach insisted.

The author sighed. "When I was younger, other kids would call me names. So I made up my own friends—monsters, demons, ghouls. And they became real to me. Then, they actually . . . *became real*. As long as the books stay locked, we're safe. But when they open . . . well, you saw what happened."

Up in Stine's office, the author froze. "One of the manuscripts is missing."

Night of the Living Dummy lay open on the floor, its lock busted.

"No," Stine said. "Not him . . ."

Evil laughter echoed through the office. "Hello, Papa."

"Slappy," Stine said, his voice shaking. "It's so nice to see you."

"Aw, shucks," Slappy said. "You're giving me . . . what's the word? *Goosebumps!*"

Stine took a step toward the dummy.

"Are you trying to put me back in?!" Slappy hissed.

"Don't be silly, Slappy." Stine stepped closer. "Just stay right there."

"I know when you're lying to me, Papa," Slappy said. The room went dark. "You've made Slappy very angry." The dummy lit a match. "He's not going back on the shelf. Ever again!"

"Slappy—don't!" Stine screamed.

Slappy tossed the match onto *Night of the Living Dummy*. "It's time I started pulling the strings in this relationship. Tonight is gonna be the best story you've ever written. *All* your children are coming out to play!"

In a flash of lightning, Slappy disappeared.

"He's gone," Stine said nervously. "And he took all the books!"

Outside, Slappy opened the lock on the *Haunted Car* manuscript. Once the car came to life, Slappy hopped inside with the other manuscripts.

The creepy dummy pawed through the locked books. "*Ooh*, this one's a real page turner!" He unlocked *Revenge of the Lawn Gnomes*.

Then he sped away in the Haunted Car, ready to make mischief.

Back inside, Stine ran down the stairs. "Out the kitchen door. Now!"

Stine and the kids ran into the kitchen— just as the lawn gnomes spilled in through the doggy flap.

"Ahhh!" Stine screeched. "Get them off me!"

Zach grabbed a broom and swung at the gnomes. The others swatted and kicked at the angry little creatures.

"Why couldn't you have written stories about rainbows and unicorns?!" Zach cried.

By the time they got past the gnomes, Slappy was long gone.

"Why is he burning the books?" Zach asked.

"So there's no way to put the monsters back inside," Stine said. "This is Slappy's revenge."

Zach pulled out his cell phone to call for help. "I can't get reception."

"Slappy's taking out all the cell towers," Stine guessed. "He's cutting us off."

On Main Street, telephone lines were down. Streetlights shattered. Statues were chewed in half. And worst of all, a dozen people were frozen in place.

"Without those manuscripts, there's nothing I can do," Stine sighed.

"If you wrote the monsters *off* the page, then there's got to be a way to write them back on the page," Zach suggested. "You need one story to capture them all."

"I need my typewriter. It's at the high school," Stine said.

Stine and the kids sped toward the high school. But suddenly, an enormous creature rose up in front of the car.

Stine slammed on the brakes. "I don't remember writing about a giant praying mantis!"

The mantis shot green mucus at the window.

"Right. Now I remember," Stine said.

"Get us out of here. Now!" Zach shrieked.

Stine slammed his foot on the gas. The car swerved. *Wham!*

As they ran away from the car, Champ cried, "Why'd you come up with something so freaky, Stine? Why?"

The kids and Stine took cover inside a grocery store. The Werewolf of Fever Swamp was chewing on a steak down one aisle. Other creatures roamed the streets outside.

"How far are we from the high school?" Zach asked.

"Not too far," Hannah said. "We can cut through the cemetery."

"A cemetery?" Zach rolled his eyes. "You've gotta be kidding me."

Across town, Slappy had set most of Stine's creatures free. A gnome hobbled toward him. "So, how did Stine die? Did he cry and beg for his life?" Slappy asked him.

The gnome said nothing. Its smile was frozen on its face.

"You couldn't kill a *writer*?!" Slappy cried. "It's like they say . . . You want something done right, you have to do it yourself!"

"If you're scared, I'll hold your hand," Zach told Hannah as they hurried through the graveyard.

Hannah laughed. "Please. You're the scaredy-cat."

Suddenly, Zach tripped on something poking out from a grave. It was a hand!

Dozens of graveyard ghouls were digging their way out of the dirt around them. Zach, Champ, Stine, and Hannah slipped through the graveyard's iron gate as the ghouls' hands grabbed at their ankles.

At the high school, they found Stine's old typewriter tucked inside a glass case.

"So, what's the story?" Stine asked.

Zach shrugged. "Monsters lose. Good guys win. The end."

Stine shook his head. "No, it won't work unless it's a real Goosebumps story: twists and turns and frights." He walked toward the auditorium. "Go to the gym and warn everyone. I'm going to find a place to write. Slappy's coming for me—I have a deadline!"

In the gym, Zach got up on stage. "Okay, monsters have invaded town."

Everyone laughed . . . until the giant praying mantis slammed its claw through the window! The laughter turned to screams.

"Calm down, everyone!" Zach shouted. "Those things out there, they're R.L. Stine's monsters. He can fix this, but we need to buy him time to write. Who here has read Goosebumps?"

Hands went up all over the gym.

Zach smiled. "Good. Then you'll all know what to do."

Monsters crashed through the doors of the school. They were under attack!

Everyone prepared to fight. Zach, Champ, and Hannah battled vampires with garlic mashed potatoes from the school cafeteria.

The football team rushed at a line of ghouls, tackling them. Kids rolled balls at the lawn gnomes, taking them down.

"Only a little longer!" Zach called. "Stine should be almost done!"

In the auditorium, Stine was stuck. "'All the monsters had come—the vampire bats, the praying mantis, the Haunted Mask . . .'"

"Forgetting somebody?" a voice rang out.

"Slappy?" Stine called.

The dummy giggled. "Work with me, and you can live. Work against me, and . . . well, you'll miss all the fun."

Slappy appeared at Stine's shoulder. "This makes Slappy . . . unhappy," he said.

The auditorium went dark. With a sick crunch, Slappy broke Stine's hands!

Zach and Hannah followed Stine's scream of pain into the auditorium. "That dummy broke my fingers!" he yelped. "I only had a page or two more."

Zach grabbed the typewriter. "We'll figure this out later. We have to get out of here!"

"Slappy wants me," Stine said. "If I can lead them away from here, I know they'll follow me—and you'll all be safe."

Zach shook his head. "I have another idea."

Ten minutes later, Slappy watched as Stine drove away in a school bus.

"Bring him to me," Slappy screamed. "Actually, just kill him."

The creatures chased after the bus. The praying mantis leaped up, landed on the bus, and flipped it on its side.

Monsters swarmed the bus. They found one of the football team's tackling dummies propped up behind the wheel.

They'd been tricked! The real Stine was getting away in a different bus!

"Where are we going?" Champ asked as he, Stine, Hannah, and Zach raced away in the other bus.

"Slappy will know wherever I go," Stine said. "We have to go somewhere I've never been. Somewhere I don't know exists."

Hannah smiled. "I know just the place."

The bus screeched to a halt outside the abandoned amusement park.

As they hurried through the park, Zach began typing the end of Stine's story.

Stine told Zach what to write: "'There was only one place in the park left to hide: the Fun House!'"

Meanwhile, Slappy was trying to write the ending of the story himself. He used his monsters to track Stine's scent. The creatures were getting closer by the minute.

"You can't hide," Slappy giggled. "Not from me, Papa."

"If you won't listen to me, Papa," Slappy said, "maybe you'll listen to"—he opened the scariest Goosebumps story of all—*"The Blob that Ate Everyone!"*

"No . . . not that. Run!" Stine screamed. He handed Zach the unfinished story. "Go! I'll hold them off. You finish the book!"

"What's the end?" Zach asked.

Stine smiled at him. "You can do this, Zach. End it."

Zach, Hannah, and Champ raced to the Ferris wheel and climbed to the top.

The Blob swallowed Stine whole. Slappy giggled. "Now *you're* trapped, Papa. This is what it feels like to be locked inside your books."

On top of the Ferris wheel, Zach was typing madly. "'Zach opened the book, and the monsters were swallowed back into the world of paper and ink . . . never to be seen again. *The end!*'"

At that moment, the praying mantis chewed through the base of the Ferris wheel. The wheel—with Zach, Hannah, and Champ inside—rolled away.

As the wheel moved, the manuscript dropped through the night sky.

But at the bottom of a hill, Champ held his arm high. "I caught it!"

Zach grabbed it. All he had to do was open it, and Stine's monsters would be sucked inside.

"I'll do it." Hannah opened the book.

There was a loud *whoosh*, and all the monsters were pulled inside.

Pop! Stine shot out of the Blob as, one by one, the monsters were sucked up.

Soon the Blob was back inside a book where it belonged. And so was Slappy.

The dummy's creepy laugh rang out one last time. "See you in your dreams, Papa!"

And so all of Stine's creatures went back where they belonged—on the shelf.

The only way to find them is to open a Goosebumps book. They're all there, waiting to take you on an adventure.

Reader, beware: You never know who might be watching and waiting for his chance to come out and play . . .